Henrietta's Hope is a timely reminder for all ages ... *Man looks at the outward appearance, but the LORD looks at the heart.* (I Samuel 16:7b) As a grandmother who enjoys reading to her young grandsons, I'm eager for more faith based stories from Hope Farm!

— *Jane (Mimi) Kehlenbeck*
Wesley and Isaac Bell

What a beautiful story told through Henrietta, which allows children to really understand that God truly has a specific plan *just for them!* Barb Hagler has taken her love for Hope Farm and allowed God to use her imagination to create a heartwarming story of God's Purposes for us.

—*Jan Baumgartner*
Children's Ministries Director
Brookside Community Church, Fort Wayne, IN

It is a sweet idea — Hope Farm — where hope is lovingly planted and harvested in season. But hope is not the only thing produced here. On Hope Farm faith and love are nurtured as well. What a wonderful series for dads and moms to read to their young children!

—Dr. William Johnson III
Pastor, Park Street Brethren Church
Ashland, Ohio

Let Henrietta's Hope encourage your child to turn their eyes upon Jesus. A winsome story, bristling with adventure, hope-filled, and amazing discovery!

—The Lambert Family,
Midland, Michigan

Henrietta's ★ HOPE ★

Tate Publishing
& Enterprises

written by
BARBARA
HAGLER

This title is also available as a Tate Out Loud product.
Visit www.tatepublishing.com for more information.

This novel is a work of fiction. However, several names, descriptions, entities, and incidents included in the story are based on the lives of real people.

The opinions expressed by the author are not necessarily those of Tate Publishing, LLC.

Published by Tate Publishing & Enterprises, LLC
127 E. Trade Center Terrace | Mustang, Oklahoma 73064 USA
1.888.361.9473 | www.tatepublishing.com

Tate Publishing is committed to excellence in the publishing industry. The company reflects the philosophy established by the founders, based on Psalm 68:11,
"The Lord gave the word and great was the company of those who published it."

Published in the United States of America
ISBN: 978-1-61566-326-2
1. Juvenile Fiction: Animals: Farm Animals
2. Juvenile Fiction: Animals: Birds
09.09.16

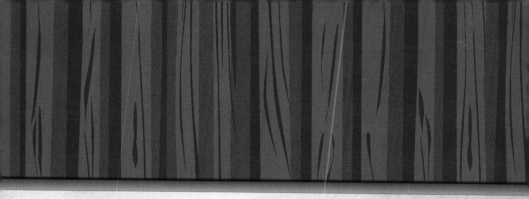

To Dan,
MY ENCOURAGER

"For I know the plans I have for you," declares the Lord, "plans to prosper you and not to harm you, plans to give you hope and a future."

Jeremiah 29:11 (NIV)

ock-a-doodle doo! Cock-a-doodle doo! crowed the rooster over the barnyard. The sound broke the silence of the morning. Hope Farm woke up.

Henrietta rustled her feathers and clucked. She wasn't ready to wake up. She was dreaming. She was beautiful. She was brown with black feathers that looked like lace around her neck. Her bright red comb crowned a beautiful … beak.

Here, she stopped. Here, she always stopped. For in her dream, her beak was straight. When she woke up, her beak was crooked.

Henrietta sighed. "I wish I could live my dream. I wish my beak was straight like every other chicken I know. Why couldn't I have a normal beak? Why did God make me this way? It must have been a mistake. But God doesn't make mistakes." Again, Henrietta sighed as she hopped out of her nest.

"Hurry, Henny! The best bugs and seeds will be gone. Remember, we have to be early birds to catch the worm," clucked Sister.

"Why hurry? I can't pick up bugs and seeds off the ground because of my—"

"—crooked beak!" finished Sister. "Yes, I know. Your crooked beak is all you talk about. At least you have a *real* name."

Yes, it was nice to have a beautiful name like Henrietta. Sister just had the name Sister. But a name could be changed. How could you change a crooked beak?

Henrietta hopped over to her tray of food. The seed was piled thick so that she could eat. It was hard to eat seeds off the ground with a crooked beak. She was thankful for the tray.

As she ate, Henrietta decided she would find a way to straighten her beak. She hopped out as soon as the farmer opened the pen. While the other chickens went to find bugs and worms, Henrietta set out to find a way to straighten her crooked beak.

Then I'll be beautiful, just like in my dream, she thought.

She found a small round hole in the side of the barn. She stuck the end of her beak into the hole and pressed her beak hard to one side, trying to straighten it.

"What-ya doing?" asked a small voice.

Not wanting to take her beak out of the hole, Henrietta replied, "Ahhm schtraitning mmy reak."

"What? Take your beak out of the side of the barn so I can understand you. Is it stuck? Let me help!" The little voice was on top of her beak, in front of her eyes. It was a mouse! The mouse tried to pull Henrietta's beak out of the hole. Henrietta's beak came out so fast it hurt!

"Ouch! Don't do that, Little Mouse!

I said I'm trying to straighten my beak!" said Henrietta as she glared at the little mouse.

"Oh, I'm sorry. I was trying to help. Mother told me to always help others." Little Mouse's ears drooped as she jumped off Henrietta's beak and scampered away.

"Wait, I'm sorry. You didn't mean to hurt me." But it was too late. Her little helper was gone. Henrietta shrugged her feathers and continued her search to straighten her beak. *That hole wasn't working anyway,* she thought.

Henrietta searched around the barnyard. She poked her beak in the woodpile, but she only knocked several logs off the pile. She rubbed her beak on a sharp rock, hoping to sand it straight. That made her beak hurt and her eyes water. When she went to get a drink from a puddle, she could see that her beak was still crooked. Henrietta hopped into the coop, tucked her beak under her wing, and closed her eyes.

"Henrietta, what is the matter?" asked Queen Victoria, a kind, white hen. "Mrs. Mouse is telling everyone in the barnyard that you yelled at Little Mouse."

"Oh," sniffed Henrietta. "I know she was trying to help, but I wanted to straighten my beak! You don't understand what it's like to have a crooked beak and not be beautiful. I can't even eat like all the other chickens. I had hoped to find a way to make it straight, but all I did was make it hurt!"

"Henrietta," clucked Queen Victoria. "You must stop thinking of yourself and what you look like. God made you special. All the hens on Hope Farm are here to provide eggs for Farmer Dan's family. We give them our best. I know you're young, but soon you'll be laying eggs too. It's time to start thinking of others."

"I'm going to lay eggs for the farmer and his family?" Henrietta perked her head to one side.

"Yes. The sooner you start eating more seeds and catching worms, the better eggs you will lay," explained Queen Victoria. "But you should apologize to Little Mouse first."

Henrietta hopped out and found the mouse. She told Little Mouse she was sorry for snapping at her.

For the next few weeks, Henrietta woke every morning with a better attitude. She had hope. Maybe God could use her even with her crooked beak. She would lay eggs to help Farmer Dan and his family, even if she had to work harder than the others because of her beak.

One day, Henrietta laid her first egg! She wasn't sure what to do. She stayed in the coop on her nest. When the farmer's wife came in to gather the eggs, she found Henrietta still on her nest.

"Henrietta, what are you doing? Did you lay an egg?" she asked as she carefully reached under Henrietta.

"Oh!" she exclaimed. In her hand, she held the most beautiful *blue* egg. "Look, Henrietta! Look at your egg. It's *beautiful!* You lay beautiful blue eggs!"

The other hens heard the farmer's wife and hopped back into the coop to see the blue egg. Queen Victoria told the young hens that Henrietta was an "Easter Egg chicken." "Some Easter Egg hens lay brown eggs, some lay green eggs, and some, like Henrietta, lay beautiful *blue* eggs," she explained.

Henrietta beamed. God hadn't made a mistake. It didn't matter that she had a crooked beak. She gave the farmer's family beautiful *blue* eggs!

Hope Farm Fun Facts

Henrietta and Sister are Araucana chickens. This breed of chicken is known to lay eggs varying in shades from turquoise to olive to brown. That is why it's called an Easter Egg chicken. We didn't know some of our chickens were Easter Egg chickens until they first started laying eggs; and suddenly, we had blue eggs. My husband thought a friend snuck into the coop and placed a dyed Easter egg in the nest as a joke! What fun Henrietta and Sister have been to our little farm in Hope, Michigan.

e|LIVE

listen|imagine|view|experience

AUDIO BOOK DOWNLOAD INCLUDED WITH THIS BOOK!

In your hands you hold a complete digital entertainment package. In addition to the paper version, you receive a free download of the audio version of this book. Simply use the code listed below when visiting our website. Once downloaded to your computer, you can listen to the book through your computer's speakers, burn it to an audio CD or save the file to your portable music device (such as Apple's popular iPod) and listen on the go!

How to get your free audio book digital download:

1. Visit www.tatepublishing.com and click on the e|LIVE logo on the home page.
2. Enter the following coupon code:
   58e9-18a9-fc80-425f-0559-7efe-20cc-afde
3. Download the audio book from your e|LIVE digital locker and begin enjoying your new digital entertainment package today!